MOTHER GOOSE
NURSERY RHYMES

ILLUSTRATED BY COLIN KING

First Published in Great Britain 1988 by
Hamlyn Publishing Group
Michelin House
81 Fulham Road
London SW3 6RB

and distributed for them by
Hamlyn Distribution Services

MOTHER GOOSE

NURSERY RHYMES

ILLUSTRATED BY COLIN KING

HAMLYN

CONTENTS

One misty, moisty morning,
When cloudy was the weather,
I chanced to meet an old man
Clothed all in leather.

He began to compliment,
And I began to grin,
How do you do, and how do you do,
And how do you do again?

6

Ride a cock-horse to Banbury Cross,
  To see a fine lady upon a white horse;
  Rings on her fingers and bells on her toes,
  And she shall have music wherever she goes.

Incy Wincy spider
Climbed up the spout.
Down came the rain
And washed the spider out.
Out came the sun
And dried up all the rain.
Incy Wincy spider
Climbed up the spout again.

Ding, dong, bell,
Pussy's in the well.
Who put her in?
Little Johnny Green.
Who pulled her out?
Little Tommy Stout.
What a naughty boy was that
To try to drown poor pussy cat,
Who never did him any harm,
And killed the mice in his father's barn.

Monday's child is fair of face,
Tuesday's child is full of grace,
Wednesday's child is full of woe,
Thursday's child has far to go,
Friday's child is loving and giving,
Saturday's child works hard for its living.
And a child that is born on the Sabbath day,
Is fair, and wise, and good, and gay.

Hush-a-bye, baby, on the tree top,
When the wind blows the cradle will rock;
When the bough breaks the cradle will fall,
Down will come baby, cradle, and all.

The north wind doth blow,
And we shall have snow,
And what will poor Robin do then?
Poor thing.
He'll sit in a barn,
And keep himself warm,
And hide his head under his wing,
Poor thing.

Cock-a-doodle-doo!
My dame has lost her shoe,
My master's lost his fiddling stick,
And knows not what to do.

Cock-a-doodle-doo!
What is my dame to do?
Till master finds his fiddling stick
She'll dance without her shoe.

Cock-a-doodle-doo!
My dame has found her shoe,
And master's found his fiddling stick,
Sing doodle-doodle-do.

Cock-a-doodle-doo!
My dame will dance with you,
While master fiddles his fiddling stick
For dame and doodle-doo.

15

Jack Sprat could eat no fat,
His wife could eat no lean,
And so between them both you see,
They licked the platter clean.

16

Little Jack Horner
Sat in the corner,
Eating a Christmas pie;
He put in his thumb,
And pulled out a plum,
And said, What a good boy am I!

I had a little nut-tree,
Nothing would it bear
But a silver nutmeg
And a golden pear;
The King of Spain's daughter
Came to visit me,
And all for the sake
Of my little nut-tree.
I skipped over water,
I danced over sea,
And all the birds in the air
Couldn't catch me.

Mary, Mary, quite contrary,
How does your garden grow?
With silver bells and cockle shells,
And pretty maids all in a row.

A was an archer, who shot at a frog;
B was a butcher, and had a great dog.

C was a captain, all covered with lace;
D was a drunkard, and had a red face.

E was an esquire, with pride on his brow;
F was a farmer, and followed the plough.

G was a gamester, who had but ill-luck;
H was a hunter, and hunted a buck.

I was an innkeeper, who loved to carouse;
J was a joiner, and built up a house.

K was King William, once governed this land;
L was a lady, who had a white hand.

M was a miser, and hoarded up gold;

N was a nobleman, gallant and bold.

O was an oyster girl, and went about town;
P was a parson, and wore a black gown.

Q was a queen, who wore a silk slip;
R was a robber, and wanted a whip.

S was a sailor, and spent all he got;
T was a tinker, and mended a pot.

U was a usurer, a miserable elf;
V was a vintner, who drank all himself.

W was a watchman, and guarded the door;
X was expensive, and so became poor.

Y was a youth, that did not love school;
Z was a zany, a poor harmless fool.

Robert Barnes, fellow fine,
Can you shoe this horse of mine?
Yes, good sir, that I can,
As well as any other man.
There's a nail and there's a prod,
And now, good sir, your horse is shod.

I had a little hen,
The prettiest ever seen;
She washed me the dishes,
And kept the house clean.
She went to the mill
To fetch me some flour,
She brought it home in
Less than an hour.
She baked me my bread,
She brewed me my ale,
She sat by the fire
And told me many a fine tale.

Baa, baa, black sheep,
Have you any wool?
Yes, sir, yes, sir,
Three bags full;
One for the master,
And one for the dame,
And one for the little boy
Who lives down the lane.

As I was going to St Ives,
  I met a man with seven wives,
  Each wife had seven sacks,
  Each sack had seven cats,
  Each cat had seven kits:
  Kits, cats, sacks and wives,
  How many were there going to St Ives?

Lavender's blue, dilly, dilly,
Lavender's green;
When I am king, dilly, dilly,
You shall be queen.

Who told you so, dilly, dilly,
Who told you so?
'Twas mine own heart, dilly, dilly,
That told me so.

Call up your men, dilly, dilly,
Set them to work,
Some to the plough, dilly, dilly,
Some to the fork.

Some to make hay, dilly, dilly,
Some to reap corn,
Whilst you and I, dilly, dilly,
Keep ourselves warm.

Roses are red, dilly, dilly,
Violets are blue;
Because you love me, dilly, dilly,
I will love you.

Hey diddle, diddle,
The cat and the fiddle,
The cow jumped over the moon;
The little dog laughed
To see such sport,
And the dish ran away with the spoon.

There was an old woman tossed up in a basket,
Seventeen times as high as the moon;
Where she was going I couldn't but ask it,
For in her hand she carried a broom.
Old woman, old woman, old woman, quoth I,
Where are you going to up so high?
To brush the cobwebs off the sky!
May I go with you? Aye, by-and-by.

Hickety, pickety, my black hen,
She lays eggs for gentlemen;
Gentlemen come every day
To see what my black hen doth lay.
Sometimes nine and sometimes ten,
Hickety, pickety, my black hen.

Hark, hark,
The dogs do bark,
The beggars are coming to town;
Some in rags,
And some in jags,
And one in a velvet gown.

London Bridge is falling down,
Falling down, falling down,
London Bridge is falling down,
My fair lady.

Build it up with wood and clay,
Wood and clay, wood and clay,
Build it up with wood and clay,
My fair lady.

Wood and clay will wash away,
Wash away, wash away,
Wood and clay will wash away,
My fair lady.

Build it up with bricks and mortar,
Bricks and mortar, bricks and mortar,
Build it up with bricks and mortar,
My fair lady.

Bricks and mortar will not stay,
Will not stay, will not stay,
Bricks and mortar will not stay,
My fair lady.

Build it up with iron and steel,
Iron and steel, iron and steel,
Build it up with iron and steel,
My fair lady.

Tom, Tom, the piper's son,
Stole a pig and away he run;
The pig was eat,
And Tom was beat,
And Tom went howling down the street.

See-saw, Margery Daw,
  Jacky shall have a new master;
  Jacky shall have but a penny a day
  Because he can't work any faster.

Pussy cat, pussy cat,
Where have you been?
I've been to London
To look at the Queen.
Pussy cat, pussy cat,
What did you there?
I frightened a little mouse
Under her chair.

36

Hickory, dickory, dock,
The mouse ran up the clock.
The clock struck one,
The mouse ran down,
Hickory, dickory, dock.

Mary had a little lamb,
  Its fleece was white as snow;
  And everywhere that Mary went
  The lamb was sure to go.

  It followed her to school one day:
  That was against the rule;
  It made the children laugh and play
  To see a lamb at school.

And so the teacher turned it out,
But still it lingered near,
And waited patiently about
Till Mary did appear.

Why does the lamb love Mary so?
The eager children cry;
Why, Mary loves the lamb, you know,
The teacher did reply.

Tweedledum and Tweedledee
Agreed to have a battle,
For Tweedledum said Tweedledee
Had spoiled his nice new rattle.
Just then flew by a monstrous crow
As big as a tar-barrel,
Which frightened both the heroes so,
They quite forgot their quarrel.

There was an old woman who lived in a shoe,
She had so many children she didn't know what to do;
She gave them some broth without any bread;
She whipped them all soundly and put them to bed.

Oh, the grand old Duke of York,
He had ten thousand men;
He marched them up to the top of the hill,
And he marched them down again.
And when they were up, they were up,
And when they were down, they were down,
And when they were only half-way up,
They were neither up nor down.

Humpty Dumpty sat on a wall,
Humpty Dumpty had a great fall.
All the King's horses and all the King's men,
Couldn't put Humpty together again.

Old Mother Hubbard
Went to the cupboard,
To fetch her poor dog a bone;
But when she got there
The cupboard was bare
And so the poor dog had none.

She went to the baker's
To buy him some bread;
But when she came back
The poor dog was dead.

44

She went to the undertaker's
To buy him a coffin;
But when she came back
The poor dog was laughing.

She took a clean dish
To get him some tripe;
But when she came back
He was smoking a pipe.

Little Polly Flinders
Sat among the cinders,
Warming her pretty little toes;
Her mother came and caught her,
And whipped her little daughter
For spoiling her nice new clothes.

Sing, sing,
   What shall I sing?
   The cat's run away
   With the pudding string!
   Do, do,
   What shall I do?
   The cat's run away
   With the pudding too!

47

Doctor Foster went to Gloucester
In a shower of rain;
He stepped in a puddle,
Right up to his middle,
And never went there again.

Rain, rain, go away,
Come again another day;
Little Johnny wants to play.

One, two,
  Buckle my shoe;

Three, four,
  Knock at the door;

Five, six,
  Pick up sticks;

Seven, eight,
  Lay them straight;

Nine, ten,
  A big fat hen;

50

Eleven, twelve,
Dig and delve;

Thirteen, fourteen,
Maids a-courting.

Fifteen, sixteen,
Maids in the kitchen;

Seventeen, eighteen,
Maids in waiting;

Nineteen, twenty,
My plate's empty.

There was a crooked man
And he walked a crooked mile;
He found a crooked sixpence
Against a crooked stile;
He bought a crooked cat
Which caught a crooked mouse,
And they all lived together
In a little crooked house.

To market, to market,
To buy a fat pig,
Home again, home again,
Jiggety-jig.
To market, to market,
To buy a fat hog,
Home again, home again,
Jiggety-jog.

Lucy Locket lost her pocket;
Kitty Fisher found it;
Not a penny was there in it,
Only a ribbon round it.

54

Goosey, goosey gander,
Whither shall I wander?
Upstairs and downstairs
And in my lady's chamber.
There I met an old man
Who would not say his prayers,
I took him by the left leg
And threw him down the stairs.

Oranges and lemons,
Say the bells of St Clement's.

You owe me five farthings,
Say the bells of St Martin's.

When will you pay me?
Say the bells of Old Bailey.

When I grow rich,
Say the bells of Shoreditch.

When will that be?
Say the bells of Stepney.

I'm sure I don't know,
Says the great bell at Bow.

Here comes a candle to light you to bed,
Here comes a chopper to chop off your head.

Hot cross buns! Hot cross buns!
One a penny, two a penny,
Hot cross buns!

If you have no daughters,
Give them to your sons,
One a penny, two a penny,
Hot cross buns!

58

This little piggy went to market,
This little piggy stayed at home,
This little piggy had roast beef,
This little piggy had none,
And this little piggy cried,
Wee-wee-wee,
All the way home.

Three little kittens
  They lost their mittens,
  And they began to cry,
  Oh, mother dear,
  We sadly fear
  Our mittens we have lost.
  What! Lost your mittens,
  You naughty kittens!
  Then you shall have no pie.
  Mee-ow, mee-ow, mee-ow.
  No, you shall have no pie.

The three little kittens
They found their mittens,
And they began to cry,
Oh, mother dear,
See here, see here,
Our mittens we have found.
Put on your mittens,
You silly kittens,
And you shall have some pie.
Purr-r, purr-r, purr-r,
Oh, let us have some pie.

Jack and Jill went up the hill,
To fetch a pail of water;
Jack fell down and broke his crown,
And Jill came tumbling after.

Then up Jack got and home did trot,
As fast as he could caper.
They put him to bed and plaster'd his head
With vinegar and brown paper.

Little Tommy Tucker
Sings for his supper.
What shall we give him?
White bread and butter.
How shall he cut it
Without e'er a knife?
How will he be married
Without e'er a wife?

63

I had a little pony,
   His name was Dapple Gray;
I lent him to a lady
To ride a mile away.
She whipped him, she slashed him,
She rode him through the mire;
I would not lend my pony now,
For all the lady's hire.

Ladybird, ladybird,
Fly away home!
Your house is on fire
And your children all gone.
All except one
And that's little Ann
And she has crept under
The frying pan.

65

Simple Simon met a pieman,
Going to the fair;
Says Simple Simon to the pieman,
Let me taste your ware.

Says the pieman to Simple Simon,
Show me first your penny;
Says Simple Simon to the pieman,
Indeed I have not any.

Simple Simon went a-fishing,
For to catch a whale;
All the water he had got
Was in his mother's pail.

Simple Simon went to look
If plums grew on a thistle;
He pricked his fingers very much,
Which made poor Simon whistle.

He went for water in a sieve
But soon it all fell through;
And now poor Simple Simon
Bids you all adieu.

Pat-a-cake, pat-a-cake, baker's man,
Bake me a cake as fast as you can;
Pat it and prick it, and mark it with T,
Put it in the oven for Tommy and me.

Rub-a-dub-dub,
   Three men in a tub,
   And how do you think they got there?
   The butcher, the baker,
   The candlestick-maker,
   They all jumped out of a rotten potato,
   'Twas enough to make a man stare.

Old King Cole
  Was a merry old soul,
  And a merry old soul was he;
  He called for his pipe,
  And he called for his bowl,
  And he called for his
    fiddlers three.

Each fiddler had a fiddle,
And a very fine fiddle had he;
Oh, there's none so rare
As can compare
With King Cole and his
  fiddlers three.

70

Hector Protector was dressed all in green;
Hector Protector was sent to the Queen.
The Queen did not like him,
No more did the King;
So Hector Protector was sent back again.

Sing a song of sixpence,
   A pocket full of rye;
   Four and twenty blackbirds,
   Baked in a pie.

When the pie was opened,
   The birds began to sing;
   Wasn't that a dainty dish,
   To set before the King?

The King was in his counting-house,
Counting out his money;
The Queen was in the parlour,
Eating bread and honey.

The maid was in the garden,
Hanging out the clothes;
When down came a blackbird
And pecked off her nose.

Little Miss Muffet
  Sat on a tuffet,
Eating her curds and whey.
There came a big spider,
Who sat down beside her
And frightened Miss Muffet away.

Cobbler, cobbler, mend my shoe,
Get it done by half past two;
Stitch it up, and stitch it down,
Then I'll give you half a crown.

Oh do you know the muffin man,
The muffin man, the muffin man,
Oh do you know the muffin man,
Who lives in Drury Lane?

Oh yes, I know the muffin man,
The muffin man, the muffin man,
Oh yes, I know the muffin man,
Who lives in Drury Lane.

Georgie Porgie, pudding and pie,
Kissed the girls and made them cry.
When the boys came out to play,
Georgie Porgie ran away.

This is the house that Jack built.
   This is the malt
   That lay in the house that Jack built.
   This is the rat,
   That ate the malt
   That lay in the house that Jack built.
   This is the cat,
   That killed the rat,
   That ate the malt
   That lay in the house that Jack built.
   This is the dog,
   That worried the cat,
   That killed the rat,
   That ate the malt
   That lay in the house that Jack built.

There was a little girl, who had a little curl
Right in the middle of her forehead;
When she was good she was very, very good,
But when she was bad she was horrid.

Six little mice sat down to spin;
Pussy passed by and she peeped in.
What are you doing, my little men?
Weaving coats for gentlemen.
Shall I come in and cut off your threads?
No, no, Mistress Pussy, you'd bite off our heads.
Oh, no, I'll not; I'll help you to spin.
That may be so, but you don't come in.

81

Yankee Doodle came to town,
Riding on a pony;
He stuck a feather in his cap
And called it macaroni.

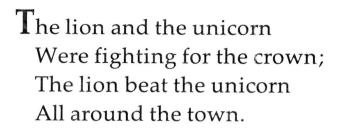

The lion and the unicorn
Were fighting for the crown;
The lion beat the unicorn
All around the town.

Some gave them white bread,
And some gave them brown;
Some gave them plum cake
And drummed them out of town.

83

The Queen of Hearts
    She made some tarts
    All on a summer's day;
The Knave of Hearts
    He stole those tarts,
    And took them clean away.

84

The King of Hearts
Called for the tarts,
And beat the knave full sore;
The Knave of Hearts
Brought back the tarts,
And vowed he'd steal no more.

Polly put the kettle on,
Polly put the kettle on,
Polly put the kettle on,
We'll all have tea.

Sukey take it off again,
Sukey take it off again,
Sukey take it off again,
They've all gone away.

Come, let's to bed,
Says Sleepy-head;
Tarry a while, says Slow;
Put on the pot,
Says Greedy-gut,
We'll sup before we go.

TUESDAY

WEDNESDAY

Solomon Grundy,
    Born on Monday,
    Christened on Tuesday,
    Married on Wednesday,
    Took ill on Thursday,
    Worse on Friday,
    Died on Saturday,
    Buried on Sunday.
    This is the end
    Of Solomon Grundy.

THURSDAY

SUNDAY

SATURDAY

FRIDAY

Pretty maid, pretty maid,
Where have you been?
Gathering roses
To give to the Queen.

Pretty maid, pretty maid,
What gave she you?
She gave me a diamond,
As big as my shoe.

89

If all the world were apple pie,
  And all the sea were ink,
  And all the trees were bread and cheese,
  What should we have for drink?

Algy met a bear,
 A bear met Algy.
 The bear was bulgy,
 The bulge was Algy.

Little Boy Blue,
   Come blow your horn,
   The sheep's in the meadow,
   The cow's in the corn.

Where is the boy
Who looks after the sheep?
He's under a haycock
Fast asleep.

Will you wake him?
No, not I,
For if I do,
He's sure to cry.

93

Boys and girls come out to play,
The moon doth shine as bright as day.
Leave your supper and leave your sleep,
And join your playfellows in the street.
Come with a whoop and come with a call,
Come with a good will or not at all.
Up the ladder and down the wall,
A half-penny loaf will serve us all;
You find milk, and I'll find flour,
And we'll have a pudding in half an hour.

Ring-a-ring o' roses,
A pocket full of posies,
A-tishoo! A-tishoo!
We all fall down.

Three young rats with black felt hats,
Three young ducks with white straw flats,
Three young dogs with curling tails,
Three young cats with demi-veils,
Went out to walk with two young pigs
In satin vests and sorrel wigs;
But suddenly it chanced to rain
And so they all went home again.

The man in the moon
Came down too soon,
And asked his way to Norwich;
He went by the south,
And burnt his mouth
With supping cold plum porridge.

Three blind mice, three blind mice!
See how they run, see how they run!
They all ran after the farmer's wife,
Who cut off their tails with a carving knife,
Did you ever see such a thing in your life,
As three blind mice?

99

Peter, Peter, pumpkin eater,
Had a wife and couldn't keep her;
He put her in a pumpkin shell
And there he kept her very well.

Peter, Peter, pumpkin eater,
Had another, and didn't love her;
Peter learned to read and spell,
And then he loved her very well.

One, two, three, four, five,
Once I caught a fish alive.
Six, seven, eight, nine, ten,
Then I let it go again.
Why did you let it go?
Because it bit my finger so.
Which finger did it bite?
This little finger on the right.

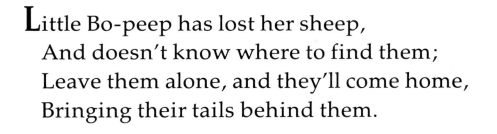

Little Bo-peep has lost her sheep,
And doesn't know where to find them;
Leave them alone, and they'll come home,
Bringing their tails behind them.

Little Bo-peep fell fast asleep,
And dreamt she heard them bleating;
But when she awoke, she found it a joke,
For they were still a-fleeting.

Then up she took her little crook,
Determined for to find them;
She found them indeed,
        but it made her heart bleed,
For they'd left their tails behind them.

It happened one day, as Bo-peep did stray
Into a meadow hard-by,
There she espied their tails side by side,
All hung on a tree to dry.

She heaved a sigh, and wiped her eye,
And over the hillocks went rambling,
And tried what she could,
        as a shepherdess should,
To tack again each to its lambkin.

Wee Willie Winkie runs through the town,
Upstairs and downstairs in his night-gown,
Rapping at the window, crying through the lock,
Are the children all in bed, for it's past
eight o'clock?

Jack be nimble,
Jack be quick,
Jack jump over
The candlestick.

105

Diddle, diddle, dumpling, my son John,
Went to bed with his trousers on;
One shoe off, and one shoe on,
Diddle, diddle, dumpling, my son John.

Up wooden hill,
Down sheet lane,
Cross pillow bank
And here we are again.

107

Twinkle, twinkle, little star,
How I wonder what you are!
Up above the world so high,
Like a diamond in the sky.

Star light, star bright,
First star I see tonight,
I wish I may, I wish I might,
Have the wish I wish tonight.

109

Index of first lines